This igloo book belongs to:

CHLOE MAMA

igloobooks

Published in 2016
by Igloo Books Ltd
Cottage Farm
Sywell
NN6 0BJ
www.igloobooks.com

GUA006 0316
2 4 6 8 10 9 7 5 3
ISBN: 978-1-78557-093-3

Illustrated by:
Lindsay Dale
Monique Dong
Flavia Sorrentino
Natasha Rimmington
Lizzie Walkly
Lilly Lazuli and Mary Bellamy

Printed and manufactured in China

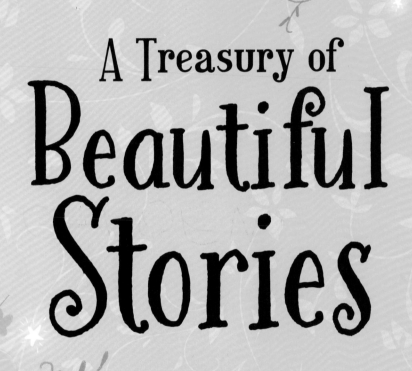

# A Treasury of
# Beautiful
# Stories

igloobooks

# Contents

# The Mermaid and the Magic Pearl

Deep down in the ocean, tucked away under a rocky shelf, there was a very special cave. Inside, hidden from most of the sea creatures, was a magic pearl. It was very large, bright and sparkling white. It rested on three gold fish under a crystal dome and every day, a sweet little mermaid named Miranda would polish it until it shone. She was the only one that knew that this pearl was a magic pearl… or so she thought.

One morning, before most merpeople were awake, Miranda swam swiftly along the seabed to the cave. She didn't see two very mischievous, fat lobsters, Larry and Lenny, following her. When she arrived, Miranda quickly looked around and then squeezed through the secret entrance. Larry and Lenny stayed very quiet and sneaked in, right behind her. They scuttled off and hid in the chamber where the pearl was kept. As Miranda began to gently polish it, she sang a little song.

"Magic Pearl, Magic Pearl, sitting on three fish. Magic Pearl, Magic Pearl, grant each special wish." The pearl glowed softly and an eerie voice said, *"Young mermaid, tell me your three wishes."* In a flash, the scheming lobsters skittered into the cave. "Hello, there," said Larry, clacking his claws loudly, distracting Miranda. "We seem to be lost. Can you show us the way out?" Miranda was so surprised that she didn't notice Lenny slip the pearl into a seaweed sack and scuttle away.

"Oh, dear," said Larry, giggling, "how very silly of me. The way out is just over there. Sorry to bother you!" and he scampered away as fast as his claws could carry him. That's when Miranda saw that the pearl was gone.

She was so upset that she swam very quickly to the royal palace and told the Merking what had happened. He stroked his beard and said, "Miranda, don't worry. I'll help you find your pearl and you will have your wishes!"

The Merking summoned two underwater detectives, Inspector Cod and PC Prawn. "Larry and Lenny Lobster have taken Miranda's magic pearl," he boomed. "You must find them and get it back!"

The two detectives nodded, bowed low and sped off. Now, Lenny and Larry were not very clever. The two of them should have scuttled away without delay. Instead, they didn't go far at all and were bragging to a shifty-looking shark about the magic pearl, when our two dashing detectives caught them red-handed!

"What have we here?" cried Inspector Cod. "Hand over that pearl, you horrible pair!" Lenny and Larry were so surprised that they gave the inspector the pearl and PC Prawn took Lenny firmly by the claw. "We only wanted to make a wish!" they wailed, as they were taken away. Back at the palace, they were still moaning. Inspector Cod gave the magic pearl to Miranda. "Shall I lock this pair away then, Your Majesty?"

Before the Merking could reply, Miranda said, "Please don't do that, Your Highness. They are very silly, but they're not really bad!" The Merking looked at Miranda and smiled. "Very well," he sighed. "But they'd better not do it again. Now, Miranda, make your first wish." Miranda closed her eyes, sang her song and wished. Suddenly, in the middle of the courtyard, a magical playground popped up, with lots of fun slides.

Miranda clapped her hands in glee. She wished again and all her friends appeared and swam towards the playground, squealing with excitement. Miranda wished one last time and the two lobsters suddenly sparkled and said, "We promise to be good from now on!" Miranda laughed and said, "Come on then. Let's go and play." All the sea creatures loved Miranda's magical playground and had fun together all that day and for many days to come. Wasn't Miranda a marvelous mermaid?

# The Littlest Fairy

Deep in the forest, hidden in the long grass, grow the fairy rings. These are special circles of toadstools and mushrooms and they are full of amazing magic. For, in a puff of smoke and a flash of light, this is where baby fairies are born. When they are very, very new, they are tiny and they hold teeny, tiny wands. The wands grow as the fairies grow. It is near one of these rings where we find Fairy Freckles.

She was so new and so tiny, that she could only fly for a short time, before she had to rest. So, she sat on a leaf in the sunshine and watched the other fairies playing. "Hello," said a voice beside her. "Are you going to the fairy ball?" Fairy Freckles turned to see a pretty fairy in a blue dress. "Hello, I'm Fairy Freckles," she said, "and I'm afraid to say that I don't know anything about the ball. When is it?"

The other fairy looked very surprised. "You don't know about the ball?" she said, in disbelief. "It's tomorrow evening and everyone is making their own dress!" She fluttered around Fairy Freckles, looking down her nose a little and showing off her hair and sparkly wings. "My name is Fairy Raindrop," said the fairy. "Meet me here tomorrow evening and you can make your dress with me and my friends." With that, she flew off, leaving poor Fairy Freckles all alone.

The next evening, Fairy Freckles was waiting on a mushroom, when Fairy Raindrop and her three friends flew up. "This is Fairy Snowflake, Fairy Moonbeam and Fairy Sunray," she said. The three fairies flew around Freckles. "You're really rather small," said Sunray, looking closely at her. "Have you made a dress before?" Fairy Freckles shook her head, shyly. "Then watch me," said Sunray. She waved her wand a few times and a beautiful, orange and pink dress suddenly appeared floating in the air.

Fairy Freckles couldn't believe her eyes. "It's the most beautiful thing I have ever seen," she sighed. "I wish it was mine."

Fairy Raindrop laughed. "You have to make your own dress. You cannot have one of ours!" she said. She swished her wand through the air. Another perfect dress suddenly floated before her. When Fairy Snowflake and Fairy Moonbeam had worked their magic, there were two more. Moonlight shone through the trees as the dresses twirled in the air.

"Now it's your turn, Freckles," said Fairy Raindrop. "Wave your wand and let's see what your dress is like!" Nervously, Fairy Freckles lifted her little wand and gave it a swish. She stared in dismay as an ordinary gray dress appeared. Her wand was too young to work properly yet! The other fairies giggled and said, "Oh, Fairy Freckles, whatever have you made?" before flying away. Fairy Freckles wiped a tear from her eye and pulled the dress from the air.

Freckles flew to the edge of the woods, where she saw an old spider, who asked her what was wrong. When Fairy Freckles told her, the spider smiled and took the gray dress. "Shall we see if I can help you?" she whispered. The spider flung the dress into the air, where it caught on her sticky web. Then, she started to spin. Thin, silvery strands of the finest thread flew into the air and swirled around the gray dress. Fairy Freckles gasped!

There, in front of her eyes, was the most sparkly dress she had ever seen. She slipped it on and hugged the spider. "Thank you so much," she said and then flew to the ball.

When she arrived, all the fairies stopped and stared. Fairy Freckles' dress was the most beautiful dress there! Raindrop, Snowflake, Moonbeam and Sunray all flew up and said they were sorry for laughing at her and being mean. Freckles forgave them and they danced together all evening!

# The Princess and the Farm

Early one morning, on a bright sunny day, Princess Melanie sat at the royal dining table, eating her breakfast. She started with a small glass of apple juice, then a large bowl of cereal with plenty of milk and finally, she ate what she loved best, a soft-boiled egg and toasted strips of bread with lots of fresh butter. She really liked dipping the toast into the runny egg, until it almost spilled out of the shell. That's when she ate it!

As Melanie sat happily eating, a sudden movement by the door that led out to the garden caught her attention. "Whatever was that?" she thought.

Melanie stood up and walked quickly to the door. She looked outside and was just in time to see a flurry of something small and yellow scuttle around a corner. She hurried after whatever it was and saw it disappear under the garden gate. So, Melanie ran to try and catch up with it.

"Excuse me! Hello!" called Princess Melanie, trying her best to stop the yellow fluffiness. At last, she rushed past the little fluffy thing and it skidded to a halt and stared at her with big, round eyes. Before she knew what was happening, it had slipped through the bushes and was speeding across the field towards a group of buildings. "I wonder who lives there?" thought Princess Melanie and she hurried along the path towards them. This was an exciting adventure!

The princess soon came to a low brick wall with a wooden gate in it.
She couldn't believe what she saw, for the little ball of fluff was perched on
the hand of a young girl about her own age and both were looking at her.
The girl walked towards her, smiling. "Hello," she said in a friendly voice.
"My name's Daisy. What's yours?"
"I'm Princess Melanie," replied the princess. "Please could you tell me
what that is?" She pointed at the fluffy, yellow thing.

Daisy laughed and held it up. "Goodness," she said, "don't you know? It's a chick and she keeps going for walks by herself when I'm not looking. She'll grow up to be a chicken. There are lots of them here on the farm." Princess Melanie looked around. "What's a farm?" she asked. "Well, this is," giggled Daisy. "This is where we keep chickens that lay eggs. There are lots of other things, too." The princess was delighted. "Please show me more." she said, as Daisy opened the gate.

"Mind your pretty shoes on the cow manure, Your Highness," said Daisy. "They'll be ruined if you don't!" Princess Melanie looked puzzled. "What is a cow?" she asked. "I've never seen one."

Daisy smiled, took her by the hand and said, "Follow me, Princess. There's so much to show you!" The pair skipped across the yard and stood by the fence in front of a big field. Princess Melanie squealed in surprise.

"These are cows," said Daisy. "This is Maisy. Hazy and Lazy are grazing across the other side of the field. They give us lovely, creamy milk. Do you have it on your breakfast cereal in the mornings?"

"Yes, I do," replied Princess Melanie, giggling, "but I didn't know where it came from. How marvelous!"

"Come on," said Daisy, "I've got another surprise for you."

In the orchard, Daisy picked up a fat chicken. "This is Henny," she said.
"She lays eggs." The princess squealed with delight.
"I love eating egg for breakfast." she said. "Daisy, will you let me come and
collect eggs and milk the cows with you and be my friend?" she asked.
Daisy said yes and so every day, the two friends had fun working on the
farm, or playing at the palace together and they lived happily ever after.

# The Mermaid and the Seahorse

Once upon a time, in a sea far, far away, there lived a pretty, little mermaid named Myrtle. Her best friend in the whole of the ocean was a seahorse named Steven. Now, Steven was a very young seahorse and sometimes, especially when he became excited, he found it very difficult to keep still. He would shoot around the seabed at top speed, leaving a long trail of bubbles behind him.

Steven wouldn't really pay attention to where he was going and before he knew it, he'd have bumped into someone and knocked them over. Quite often, he was going so fast that he would whizz by and not stop. Myrtle was forever helping people up and saying, "I really am so sorry about Steven." Quite often, Steven would break things and then he really got a scolding, but he wasn't a bad seahorse. He was just far too fast and enthusiastic for his own good.

One day, Steven and Myrtle were playing bubble-ball by some rocks. Myrtle threw the ball hard and it zoomed over Steven's head. He sped after it, but didn't see Ozzie Octopus, who was carrying a huge pile of shells, until it was too late. BAM! Ozzie went flying through the water and his shells scattered everywhere. He wiggled his legs angrily and shouted, "Myrtle, something has to be done about Steven!" he said, angrily.

"Last week, he knocked Lucy Lobster over and bruised her claw, then he smashed the big sandcastle that Cornelius Crab had made for his daughters. He's causing too much trouble!"

Suddenly, Ozzie had a wonderful idea. "I know," he said. "You should take him to the Seahorse Races at Ocean City, Myrtle. That's one place where he could swim as fast as he liked and no one would moan."
"Oh, Ozzie, you are clever!" squealed Myrtle.

So, the next weekend, Steven and Myrtle went to the races, along with a lot of the poor creatures that Steven had knocked over. The racecourse was buzzing with all sorts of folks. There were big, moody sharks, silly starfish and even a whale! Myrtle and Steven had never seen such a crowd. They went to the starting line and Steven was entered into the first race by a large prawn named Gerald, who seemed to be in charge.

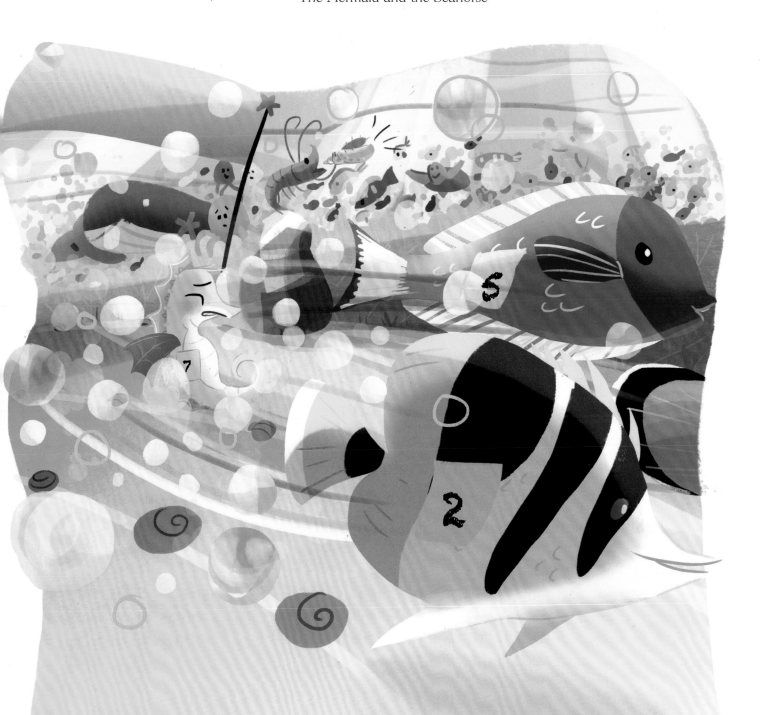

When the competitors were ready, Gerald blew on a large seashell and the race was off! Steven shot forward, but he was bowled over in a flurry of bubbles made by the big fish beside him. This had never happened to him before and it was horrible. This must be how it felt when he knocked others over. How awful! He set off again, but he was far behind. Then, at the next bend, he could see Myrtle and his friends.

Steven could see that they were waving and cheering loudly. He decided right then that he was going to win the race just for them. He curled up his tail and shot ahead so fast that he made the water swirl behind him. He sped past a couple of clownfish and a butterfly fish, who was getting very tired. The crowd was yelling louder and now, there was only one shiny shark ahead of him. Steven was right on his tail.

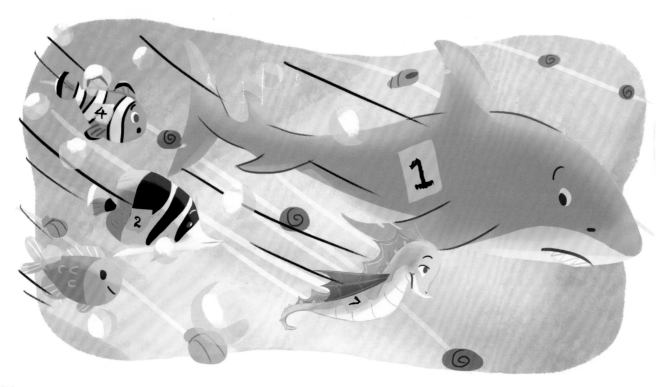

Two seconds later, the shark was so surprised to see Steven overtaking him, that he hiccupped and stumbled and Steven flew over the finish line. Hurray, he had won by a nose!

Myrtle swam up and hugged Steven and everyone clapped and cheered when he was presented with the Winners' Cup. He looked around and grinned and said, "Thank you all for supporting me and I promise you all that from now on, I'll try to only rush in races!"

# The Fairies and the Sudden Surprise

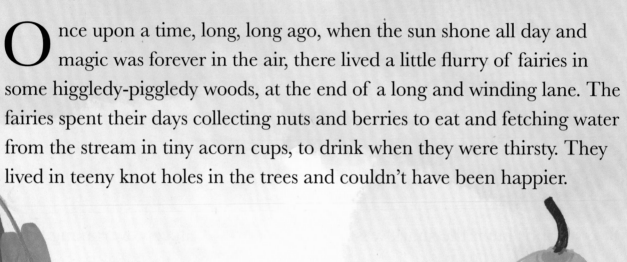

Once upon a time, long, long ago, when the sun shone all day and magic was forever in the air, there lived a little flurry of fairies in some higgledy-piggledy woods, at the end of a long and winding lane. The fairies spent their days collecting nuts and berries to eat and fetching water from the stream in tiny acorn cups, to drink when they were thirsty. They lived in teeny knot holes in the trees and couldn't have been happier.

The most important thing that the fairies did, though, was to help and look after the small creatures that also lived in the woods. Fairy Twinkle was great at caring for frogs and toads and Fairy Sparkle just loved to lend Mrs. Beetle a hand with her beautiful baby beetles. In fact, all of the fairies, Fairy Sunshine, Fairy Moondust, Fairy Flora and Fairy Fauna made sure that Stickleback Woods was a wonderful place to live.

There was one fairy who would sleep most of the time. She was named Fairy Slumber and she was very, very old. When she was awake, she would tell stories to the fairies about days gone by. Fairy Slumber had seen the woods grow from tiny seedlings into the tall trees that towered there now. The fairies loved to hear her tales, but quite often, Fairy Slumber would drop off to sleep before she finished telling them the ending!

Moondust House

For many years, the folks of Stickleback Woods, animals and little fairies, lived happily together. Then, one day, a cloud crossed the setting sun and there was a sudden chill in the air. The fairies were very worried. "What's happening?" asked Fairy Sunshine, but no one knew.

The fairies all fluttered off to bed, as night fell. Fairy Moondust suddenly remembered she'd left her wand at Squirrel's house, so she flew back to fetch it and that's when something big and white bumped into her.

Fairy Moondust looked up into the dark sky and gasped, as millions of sparkling, white crystals tumbled down. "Oh, dear!" she cried out, feeling very afraid. "The sky is falling down!" She swiftly flew to Fairy Slumber's home, calling the other fairies to follow her as she went. Soon, they all stood on the old fairy's doorstep, as Fairy Moondust knocked on the door. It opened and they all started to talk at once, but stopped when suddenly, Fairy Slumber said, "Oh, look! It's snowing!"

"It hasn't snowed for a hundred years," sighed Fairy Slumber. "It won't hurt you, my dear fairies. Snowflakes are gentle. Use your magic to fly amongst them and see." The fairies looked up, waved their wands and flew into the air. The snowflakes flittered down and the fairies sped around and around them, laughing and enjoying themselves, until they were all completely tired out. "Off to bed now, little ones," said Fairy Slumber. "In the morning, there will be lots more excitement!"

Next day, the air was filled with a strange, bright light and when the fairies looked out on Stickleback Woods, it was covered in a blanket of white fluff. In seconds, they were outside, rolling around and sparkling with snow. They laughed and made snowballs, giggling as they threw them at one another. Fairy Sunshine waved her wand and up popped a snowfairy! Later, they made a slide and glided along at top speed. By nightfall, they were all ready for bed.

The following morning, the sun shone brightly and the fairies were all ready for more fun. To the fairies' great surprise, the snow was nearly gone. "It has melted," said Fairy Slumber. "Don't worry though, it will snow again one day and we can all enjoy it once more. The fairies were a little sad that the snow had gone. They wished that it would come again soon and if they were lucky, maybe they wouldn't have to wait a hundred years!

# The Messy Princess

Once upon a time, in a land not so very far away, there lived a king and a queen. They had a daughter, named Princess Georgina. She was no ordinary princess. In fact, some people thought she was very unusual. You see, Princess Georgina did not like pretty dresses and she hated sparkly shoes. If anyone tried to comb her hair, she would throw a temper tantrum and everyone was scared of her.

What Princess Georgina liked best was to wear her old, blue jeans with the rips in them, her raggedy T-shirt and best of all, her muddy, red sneakers. When she woke up in the morning, she ignored her maid who held up a nice girlie dress and rushed to put her choice of clothes on before anyone could make her dress up. Once she was wearing them, no one could get her to change her clothes, not even the king or queen.

Then, one morning, Princess Georgina woke up to find her usual clothes were missing. In their place was a pink satin dress, a pair of pink shoes and worst of all, a tiara! She hated wearing tiaras.

Her mother, the queen, stood by her bed. "Now, Georgina," she said. "Your father and I want you to wear your very best clothes today. King Michael and Queen Susan are coming to visit and I want you to be a very good girl. Do NOT get dirty, whatever you do!"

Princess Georgina got out of bed. With the queen's help, she put on the
pink satin dress and the pink shoes. The queen tried her best to comb the
princess's hair, but when it kept springing back, she gave up. She fixed
the little tiara on her daughter's head and said, "Now, dear, go down
to the dining room and have your breakfast and do try your very best
to stay clean." Princess Georgina was not happy. She glared at her
mother and stomped off.

Princess Georgina clomped down the stairs. She really didn't want to wear this horrible dress. She sat down to eat her breakfast and in no time at all, she had splashed cereal and milk on her dress, smudged egg in her hair and dragged her sleeve through the jam. Georgina tried to wipe it off, but that just seemed to make it worse. Maybe her mother and father wouldn't notice. "Come on, Rags, let's go outside," said the princess to her little dog, as she jumped down from her chair.

Princess Georgina, followed by Rags, ran through the palace gardens towards the orchard, racing as fast as she could. What a shame that she didn't see the puddle until it was too late. Sploosh!

Now her new shoes were covered in mud. Maybe her mother and father wouldn't notice. Suddenly, Georgina spotted her kite, stuck high up in an apple tree. "Hey, Rags," she yelled. "Let's rescue my kite!" and she began to climb the tree.

The princess climbed and climbed, but she couldn't reach the kite. A branch caught on her dress and tore a big hole in it. "Oh, dear!" said Georgina, as a twig messed her hair up and another caught onto her tiara and knocked it off. Now she was truly stuck.

"Rags," called Georgina, as loud as she could. "Go and get help!" Rags ran off and soon came back with a gardener, who was carrying the royal ladder. In no time at all, the princess was on the ground again.

Suddenly, Princess Georgina heard the sound of the royal trumpet. The visitors had arrived. She and Rags ran as fast as they could and arrived just in time, but Princess Georgina did look quite messy. What would their royal visitors think?

King Michael and Queen Susan stepped from the carriage. Young Prince George came next and ran past them to say hello. To Georgina's delight, she saw that he was just as messy as she was!

"Would you like to come and play with me and Rags?" asked Georgina. "Oh, yes please!" replied the prince and he and Princess Georgina and Rags the dog ran off towards the palace gardens at top speed. They had fun splashing in muddy puddles and rolling down grassy banks. They ate apples from the trees and swung on ropes over the stream.

When they were tired, Princess Georgina and Prince George went back to the palace and they looked so happy that their parents simply couldn't scold them.

When King Michael said it was time to go home, Princess Georgina said, "Thank you for being just as messy as me. Come and play again soon!"
"I will," replied Prince George, happily and he waved as they drove away.

# The Mermaid and the Gold Comb

Long ago, when the world was still new, a young mermaid named Merrily lived in the castle of the Merqueen. The old queen was very fond of Merrily and spent hours telling her of days gone by. "My hair was as bright as the morning sun," she said one day. "I would spend hours sitting on the rocks by the seashore, combing it until it shone. All the other mermaids would stare, it was so beautiful."

The old queen reached down and ran her fingers through Merrily's
long gold hair. "You remind me so much of myself, my dear, when I
was your age. Would you like to see what made my hair so very special?"
Merrily nodded and the queen reached down into a silver chest and
took out a gold comb. It sparkled in the light. "Let me show you what
it can do," she whispered, as she gently ran it through Merrily's hair.

Merrily looked into a hand mirror and gasped. Where the old queen had combed her hair, it had turned a glossy, sparkling pink. The queen did it again and her hair turned blue. Merrily laughed and said, "That is a wonderful comb, Your Majesty."

The queen stared into her eyes and murmured, "I want you to have it, Merrily, but you must promise to keep it safe, for strange things will come to pass if anything bad happens to it."

Merrily thanked the queen and hugged her tightly. "I promise I'll keep it safe, Your Majesty," she said as she took the comb and swam away.

At home, Merrily looked in the mirror and carefully combed her hair. She thought of green and suddenly her hair was green! Merrily didn't notice another mermaid, named Sally, watching her at the window.

Now, Sally really wanted to try the comb and she swam away as fast as she could to tell her friends. So, when Merrily came swimming by with her shining, green hair, Sally and some little mermaids were waiting for her. "Great hair, Merrily," said Sally. "Can I try your comb?"

Merrily was very surprised to see the mermaids and said, "What are you talking about, Sally? I don't know what you mean."

"Don't pretend you don't know," said Sally. "I saw you with a magic comb. It's probably in your bag now." She swam forward and grabbed the bag so that everything inside it fell out. The gold comb flew through the water and hit a large rock, where it smashed into seven pieces. Sally and her friends swam past Merrily and before she could do anything, they were each holding a piece of the comb, running it through their hair.

In a moment, each girl's hair had changed. They laughed, swapped combs and in seconds, their hair was another shade. Merrily sobbed. The mermaids had broken her lovely comb. The queen would be furious!

Merrily was very sad, but before she could say anything, a deep rumbling shook the water and suddenly, the Merqueen appeared before them. "Mermaids, you have broken my precious comb," she boomed, pointing at Sally and her friends. "Now you must put things right!"

"From now on, whenever there is a storm over the ocean, you will rise from the water and comb the raindrops, until a rainbow appears! Do you understand me?" said the queen, angrily. The mermaids nodded. "We are very sorry, Your Majesty," they said and swam away, quickly. "Come, Merrily," said the queen, gently. "I have a brush you might like at the castle," and off they went.

So, when it rains over the ocean and you spy a rainbow, look closely and see if you can spot the seven mermaids, combing the rain!

# The Fairy and the Three Wishes

Once upon a time, in the countryside near a stream, there lived a pretty, little fairy. Her name was Fairy Sunshine and everyone who met her, loved her. One day, she was flying by a meadow of gold corn, when she came upon a dormouse who looked upset. "Mr. Dormouse, whatever is wrong with you?" asked Fairy Sunshine, kindly.

"I've hurt my foot," sniffled the dormouse, twitching his whiskers. "And I have SO much to do!"

Fairy Sunshine looked at his foot, which was very pink and looked sore.
"Where were you going to?" she asked, cheerfully. The dormouse sighed.
"I was going to the stream to fetch water," he whispered. "But my foot
hurts too much." Fairy Sunshine picked up his little acorn-cup pail.
"I will get it for you," she said, gently. She flew to the stream and,
in seconds, gathered the water and sped back to the dormouse.
He was so pleased that he hugged her.

Fairy Sunshine flew on through the corn. Suddenly, she saw a bird hopping around, trying to drag a large twig through the dirt. He looked very tired and was having great difficulty moving it. "Hello, Mr. Bird," said Fairy Sunshine, sweetly. "What are you doing?"

"I'm trying to take this twig to the nest I'm building," replied the bird, but I have hurt my wing and cannot fly."

"Please let me help," said the fairy and she fluttered over to a bush and picked up as many twigs as she could possibly carry.

Sunshine flew back to the little bird and then they both went to his nest, where she laid down the twigs. "You are SO kind," tweeted the bird. "Thank you very much for all your help."

A short time later, Fairy Sunshine fluttered over a grassy bank that was filled with beautiful flowers. Suddenly, she heard a sneeze and saw a very sad honeybee sitting on a flower, with gold pollen dust sprinkled all around her. "Whatever is the matter, Mrs. Honeybee?" asked the fairy.
The honeybee sniffed and replied, "Well, I've got a cold and every time I dip into a flower to collect pollen, I seem to sneeze and the pollen falls off! Just look at all this mess."

Fairy Sunshine saw the spilled pollen. "Well, dear Mrs. Honeybee, I am just on my way to school right now," she said, "but I can spare a few minutes to help you collect some pollen." She picked up a dandelion flower and flew around the bank, dipping it in and out of the blooms. After a while, the dandelion was full of pollen. Mrs. Honeybee was thrilled. "Thank you, Fairy Sunshine," she said, giving a big smile. "That is so kind of you!"

Fairy Sunshine flew as fast as she could to fairy school. She had a special test that morning and arrived just in time. The teacher said that the fairy with the best mark would get three wishes as her prize. So, Fairy Sunshine tried very hard and to her delight, she got the top mark! She told her class all about her journey to school and the little creatures that she had tried to help. "So, this is what I want to wish for," she said.

"I wish that Mr. Dormouse didn't have a wounded foot and Mr. Bird's wing wasn't hurt and Mrs. Honeybee didn't have a cold."

The teacher waved her wand and told Fairy Sunshine that all her wishes were granted. She also said that she was going to give Fairy Sunshine another wish, as she was so kind to others. Sunshine was so pleased that she wished for a party for all her school friends. What a very special fairy Sunshine was!

# The Princess Who Wanted a Pet

Princess Olivia really wanted a pet. She pestered her mommy and daddy all the time, but they just said no. One sunny morning, the king and queen were sitting in their deckchairs, admiring their garden, when Princess Olivia leaped from behind a bush and made them jump. "Olivia!" shrieked the queen. "Whatever is the matter?" Princess Olivia laughed, climbed onto her daddy's lap and gave him a big hug.

"Please may I have some friends over for tea tomorrow?" she asked, smiling sweetly.

The king, who was named Jeremy, was trying to enjoy a snack. He mumbled something and nodded, so Princess Olivia gave him a big kiss and said, "Oh, thank you, Daddy." She ran off towards the palace as fast as her legs could carry her, before the queen had a chance to say no.

You see, Princess Olivia had a plan. This wasn't going to be any ordinary sort of tea party. It was going to be a 'Bring your Pet Along' tea party, but it was a secret.

When Olivia reached her bedroom, she found paper and pens and began to write out all the invitations. She wrote in the middle of each page, 'Please come to Princess Olivia's Pet Party tomorrow at 3 o'clock! Do not come if you can't bring your pet!' and drew lots of little pictures of pets around the edges. Then, she addressed them carefully with her best pens. When they were all done, she called a page boy and told him to deliver them to all of her friends.

The next day, the royal cook made lots of tasty sandwiches and cakes. By 3 o'clock, Princess Olivia was welcoming her guests. The first was a boy named Roger. He held a covered cage in his hand. "Hello, Princess," he said. "I'll show you my pet after tea!" He rushed over to the table and quickly gobbled two sandwiches. Princess Olivia thought he was rather rude, but she didn't have time to say anything then, because her other guests arrived.

Suddenly, the room filled with children and pets. Paula had brought
a very sleek cat with a pink bow around its neck and John was carrying
a jar with a stick insect in it. Over by the door, Emily was petting the
feathers of a gorgeous parrot, which was beginning to whistle and sitting
by the fireplace was Madeleine, whose pet was a very cute penguin! A boy
named William was chasing a mischievous monkey, which stole a sandwich
and ran off.

Princess Olivia clapped her hands and said, "Thank you to all of you for coming today. My mommy and daddy will be here in a minute to see your wonderful pets. Then, they might let me have one of my own. Now, let's all have tea!"

Everyone sat at the table and ate quietly. Then, Princess Olivia asked Roger to show her his pet and that's when the trouble started.

Inside the cage was a huge spider. Paula, Emily and Madeleine let out piercing screams. The cat escaped from Paula's arms and ran up the curtains and the parrot flew away from Emily and landed on the mantelpiece, squawking loudly. The monkey shrieked and dropped the sandwiches and the penguin leaped into the jelly. Only John's stick insect remained calm. It was at that moment that the king and queen arrived. Princess Olivia gasped!

There in the king's arms was the cutest puppy she had ever seen.
All the pets and children looked at him. "Oh, Mommy and Daddy,"
cried Olivia, "is he for me?" The king put the puppy in her arms
and said, "We heard that your party was for pets and we didn't want you
to be left out. His name is Rover." Princess Olivia hugged Rover and said,
"Thank you so much! He's the best pet in the world!"

# The Mermaid and the Shark

Once upon a time, there lived a little mermaid named Molly. Her home was on the edge of a deep lagoon, in a beautiful cave, which she shared with her mom, dad and her two sisters. There were several more caves nearby and there were other merfolk living in them, too. In fact, it was a very happy little village. Every day, all the young merchildren played together and had fun. They even enjoyed going to the merschool.

There were lots of other sea creatures that lived there too, but everyone seemed to get along just fine. Molly, her sisters and friends loved to play, especially hide-and-seek. They all thought it was the very best game. Molly was very good at it and she always knew the best places to hide.

Then, one beautiful morning, a new family arrived. They were Mr. and Mrs. Shark, who were lovely and their young son, Simon, who was not.

Simon Shark was very, very badly behaved and it didn't take Molly and all her friends long to find this out. The day after the Sharks moved in to the village, the children were all sitting down in the marketplace, making shell pictures when… WHOOOSH! Simon swam right through the middle of them all, swishing his tail and smashing all their lovely pictures. Oh, how he laughed! The smaller children started to cry, but Molly was just really angry.

The next day, Molly and her sisters were making sandcastles, when Simon swooped down from above and knocked them over. He sat down on the ocean floor and laughed and laughed. "You should see your silly faces," said Simon. "You look so funny!" Molly was really fed up.

"Simon, you have spoiled our fun," she said. "Why don't you come and play with us, instead of being horrible?" Simon just stuck out his tongue and sped away.

Over the next few days, Simon Shark did his best to upset Molly the mermaid and her friends as often as he could. He filled their school bags with stinky seaweed and dropped jellyfish on their heads. He tied Molly's tail to a rock and chased her sisters until they squealed. When they tried to talk to him, he just blew bubbles at them and that was when Molly had a terrific plan. She told everyone about it.

The very next day, Molly was swimming around in front of Simon's house by herself, singing. When he saw her, she shouted, "Bet you can't catch me!" and swam off as fast as she could.

Simon, of course, couldn't resist a challenge and in no time at all, he swam out of his home and followed Molly. He chased her through the deep, sea caves, past clumps of seaweed and through coral reefs, but he couldn't catch her. That's when Molly's plan came into action.

Molly swam through a hole in a big rock. Simon swam after her and as he did so, he felt something tighten around his middle and heard a funny tinkling sound. The clever mermaids had tied a bell on a piece of rope and now, it was firmly stuck around his tummy! No matter how hard he tried, he couldn't shake it off. He was so angry. The mermaids just watched him swishing around in circles and started to laugh.

So, whenever the friends heard the tinkling bell, they knew that Simon was near and were ready for whatever mischief he might be planning. Simon couldn't scare them anymore. He was fed up of hearing the bell all the time and at last, he said sorry to Molly and her friends. "Please, Molly, take the bell off and I promise never to be bad again," he said.

So, Molly removed the bell and they all played happily together from then on, with no more of Simon's mischief!

# The Fairy Who Bent Her Wand

Fairy Dewdrop sat on her wand and bent it! Oh, no, whatever was she going to do? She wasn't very good at spells. She'd always managed to get by, but now that her wand was bent, anything could happen. Dewdrop gave her wand a flick and blue sparks shot out of it. Instead of going straight, they flew around the corner. Dewdrop went to see what had happened, and found that the cabinet had sprouted wings and was trying to fly!

Slowly, Dewdrop raised the wand again and gave it a little swish. As she did, silver sparks shot out of it, then swerved around the corner. When she went to look where they'd gone, a big, fat hen was staring up at her, where before there had been a stool. "Oh, shoot," said Fairy Dewdrop, angrily. "That was supposed to be a pink hat!" It seemed she could only do magic around corners now and she couldn't do that very well!

Fairy Dewdrop shooed the hen outside. Maybe she'd better try again? She stood really still, thought very hard and waved her wand up and down quickly. Red sparks shot out, curved to the left, flew out of the window and hit a tree! It instantly sprouted hundreds of frying pans. What a terrible time for her wand to stop working! Tomorrow, Dewdrop was going to the royal palace to fix the king's broken fountain. How could she do that now?

The next morning, Fairy Dewdrop was standing by the fountain in the royal courtyard with her wand in her hand. She was wearing her best dress and her wings were shining in the sunlight. The king and all his royal attendants were gathered around, for everyone wanted to see Dewdrop make the fountain work again. She'd been very excited yesterday, but now she was just worried. Dewdrop decided not to tell the king there was a problem. She'd simply hope for the best.

Fairy Dewdrop closed her eyes tightly and flicked her wand three times in the air. She opened one eye, but nothing seemed to have happened. She was about to try again, when she felt a rumbling underground.

"Oh, this is not good," she whispered. Suddenly, bright gold sparks shot out of the fountain. The sparks quickly turned into a flock of birds, which dived at the attendants. In an instant, there was a loud POP! and the birds vanished. Then, there came another rumble!

With an enormous SPLAT, a spurt of chocolate milkshake erupted from the top of the gold fountain. Now, as this was a magic milkshake, it didn't just go up in the air and then straight down again. It actually seemed to chase after the attendants, who ran in all directions, as they tried to get away. The magic milkshake didn't want to let them escape, though and swooped after them, until it had gathered them around the fountain. Everyone held their breath. SWOOOOSH!

Tomato soup, thick and red and creamy, sprayed from the fountain and splashed down over the crowd. At the same time and to everyone's surprise, the fountain began to sing. Fairy Dewdrop wiped soup from her face and looked for the king. Now, the king was a sensible man. He was standing to one side under a large umbrella, which he'd brought with him in case it rained. He was laughing so much that tears were running down his cheeks.

"Oh, Fairy Dewdrop," boomed the king, "that's the funniest thing I've ever seen. Why do you look so sad?"

Fairy Dewdrop told the king the whole story, without leaving anything out. When she'd finished, the king looked at her with a twinkle in his eye and then he said, "I know just who can help you." He waved his hand and an attendant, who was still dripping with soup and milkshake, came forward. The king whispered something in his ear and the attendant ran off.

"Come along with me," said the king to Fairy Dewdrop. "We'd better get you cleaned up. We will be having a special visitor coming soon and you cannot meet her looking like that!" They went into the palace, followed by the dripping attendants, who were very upset and grumbling. They had never seen anything like it in all their lives! What a mess!

When everyone was clean, they gathered in the courtyard again, just in time for their special visitor to fly in.

It was the Fairy Queen! When she heard what had happened, she called Fairy Dewdrop forward. "Show me your wand," she said. The nervous fairy stepped forward and held out her wand. When the Fairy Queen touched it with her own wand, the bend disappeared completely. "Try your wand now," she said. Fairy Dewdrop waved it at the fountain and clear, bright water whooshed out of it! The king and all the attendants cheered and after that, Fairy Dewdrop was careful never to sit on her wand again!

# The Princess and the Treasure

There was once a little princess, called Iris. She lived in a splendid palace with her mommy and daddy, the king and queen. One day, Princess Iris was playing in the great hall with some of her friends. They really wanted to play outside, but it was raining. They had drawn pictures and dressed up their dolls and now they were just bored. "I'm going to dance," said Princess Iris and began to whirl and spin around in her beautiful dress, as if she were at a royal ball.

Princess Iris began to feel dizzy. As she twirled around, she didn't see the shiny suit of armor until it was too late. She banged into it and knocked it over with a CRASH! Now, the suit of armor was holding a spear and this spear hit a wooden panel in the wall very hard and before anyone could speak, the panel opened like a door! Princess Iris and her friends rushed to the opening and peered in. Whatever could be behind it?

Behind the panel, the friends could see a winding staircase going down. The girls fetched some lanterns and climbed through the opening. It smelled old and damp. Very, very slowly, they made their way down, down the steps, being very careful not to slip. It was very cold and they could see their breath in the air. Oh, how they wished they'd brought their coats with them! Just then, a loud scream echoed around the tunnel!

Princess Iris and her friends jumped with fright and then turned to see what had happened. There, at the back of the line, was Emily and she was staring at an enormous, furry spider. Emily watched as it scuttled off and she shuddered. "Sorry," she whispered. "I didn't mean to scream, but it frightened me." The friends sighed with relief and continued down the winding, stone steps. They hadn't gone far when there was another scream.

This time it was Jenny who screamed. "A wet thing dropped on my nose!" she cried, as she touched it. They all looked up and saw water drops falling from the stone ceiling above their heads. The friends began to laugh. It was very easy to be scared in the secret tunnel.

Princess Iris turned to continue on and then she squealed. There right in front of her face, on a little ledge, was a fat, brown mouse. Its ears shot up in fright and it scampered away. He was scared, too!

The girls continued on down and suddenly, they were in the most fabulous room they had ever seen. It was stacked from floor to ceiling with gold and jewels. The girls couldn't believe their eyes! They rushed in and began to look around. Princess Iris giggled as she danced around with Emily and Jenny, while Charlotte stared at the glittering treasure in amazement.

Before long, they were all wearing gold crowns, silver tiaras, necklaces, earrings of precious jewels and lots of rings. They all began to dance, swirling their dresses and laughing as they went. There was a big gold chair by one wall and Princess Iris said, "I'm the queen of the treasure kingdom and this is my throne!" and down she sat. Suddenly, the wall behind the princess slid away, revealing a corridor in the palace where the king and queen were walking.

Iris's parents couldn't believe their eyes. They had never seen so much beautiful treasure! "Iris, my dear," said the king, "how did you find all this royal gold? This is the family fortune that we thought was lost forever."

Princess Iris told him the whole story. The king and queen laughed and were overjoyed. They couldn't believe their luck and the little princess said, "I'll never think playing in the palace is boring ever again!"

# The Mermaid Who Couldn't Swim

Once upon a time, in a sea far away, there lived a little mermaid named Elsa. No matter how hard she tried, poor Elsa just could not swim properly! You might think that it was impossible for a mermaid not to be able to swim, but Elsa only had to flick her tail even the teensiest, tiniest bit and she would flip right over and tumble into a heap on the seabed. It happened every time and it made Elsa very sad.

You see, unless she held on to something, Elsa's head always sank
downwards and her tail floated upwards and nothing that anyone did made
it better. Poor Elsa could never go out on her own. One of her friends or
family had to go with her to hold her upright. Elsa didn't like this at all,
for it meant that she was never able to play outside by herself.
It wasn't long before everyone had just about had enough.

It nearly always fell to Elsa's mom to take her outside. Her brothers and sisters were far too busy playing with their friends to be bothered with their sister. So, she would sit on a rock, hold on tight and watch them play and chase each other. It really wasn't much fun for her. Oh, how Elsa longed for the day when she could swim. Then, she could join in all the fun and games and splash around with her friends.

Now, one morning, Elsa's mom was in quite a hurry. She had so much to do that she wasn't really paying attention to Elsa, who was going to the store with her. As she swam, poor Elsa was nosediving into the sand every few seconds and it was starting to hurt. "Oh, Elsa," said her mom, turning around, "I think it's about time I took you to see the doctor. Maybe he will know what to do with you!"

The doctor was a white-haired merman, with a very large tummy.
He watched as Elsa flopped and flipped all over his office. He scratched his
head, looked at her tongue and into her ears. "I know exactly what
is wrong," he said to Elsa's mom. "You need to buy her blue seaweed.
It is very expensive, but she needs to eat a handful, three times a day,
for a week. Then, she will be able to swim just like everyone else!"

So, poor little Elsa ate the sticky, chewy, blue seaweed, three times a day, for a whole week. It tasted absolutely disgusting! In fact, she decided that it was easily the worst thing she had EVER put in her mouth. She swallowed it down, though, because she wanted to swim just like her brothers and sisters.

You can imagine how upset Elsa was when, one week later, she tried to swim on her own and nosedived into the sand again!

Elsa was very upset and so were her family and friends. They had all gathered to watch her first real swim. Also there, but floating at the back of the crowd, was Octavius Octopus, who was very old and very, very wise. He saw how upset Elsa was and as everyone swam away, he slowly wiggled over to Elsa's mom and whispered in her ear.

Elsa's mom beamed at Octavius, gave him a huge hug and then swam off towards the store.

Ten minutes later, she returned with a package, smiling cheerfully. She swam into her cave and shut the door. Whatever had Octavius said?

The next day, Elsa and her mom came out of their cave and everyone who saw them couldn't believe their eyes.

For Elsa was swimming upright, just like all the other mermaids… and wearing a beautiful pair of bright pink water wings on her arms. Fantastic! Now Elsa could join in all the games and be just like her friends.

# The Fed Up Fairy

Fairy Isabelle was really fed up. Ever since she had woken up that morning, her mommy had given her so many jobs to do that she hadn't had a moment to herself. She'd dusted the knick-knacks on the sitting room buffet and she'd polished the table in the hall until it shone like a jewel. Isabelle had even hung out all of the wet laundry and there had been so much of it, she'd had to use next door's clothesline, as well!

Now, Isabelle was sitting on a big toadstool, trying to catch her breath for a moment in the warm sunshine. She had wanted to play with her friends, but her mommy had asked her to stay and help and that was why she was fed up. She was sure her friends were all enjoying themselves without her. Not one of them had come by to see if anything was wrong and that made Fairy Isabelle even more fed up!

"Isabelle, come here will you, please?" called her mommy. Fairy Isabelle frowned and hoped that there were no more jobs to do. If there were, she was quite sure that she would be the most fed up fairy in the forest! To her surprise, her mommy said, "All the jobs are done now, Isabelle. Change your dress and then you can fly off and play with your friends!" Fairy Isabelle changed quickly and flew out through the door.

Isabelle flew as fast as her wings could carry her to the house of her friend, Fairy Primrose. She knocked several times on the door, but no one seemed to be in. Suddenly, a very grumpy goblin looked out of a window in a nearby tree and shouted, "She's not in and stop making all that noise!" He slammed his window and Fairy Isabelle flew off quickly. She tried at Mole's house, but an earthworm wearing big glasses said that Mole was out.

Fairy Isabelle was even more fed up now. She flew up into the air and then, suddenly thought she heard music and laughter in the breeze. She landed softly on a branch and listened, but whatever she had heard had stopped. So, Isabelle flew on and arrived at Mrs. Bunny's burrow. A card pinned to the door announced 'Gone out' and moments later, when she fluttered down to Fairy Dimple's house, she found that no one was at home.

Isabelle wondered where her friends could be and why had none of them come to call for her? She really did feel quite upset and perched on a long leaf to wipe away a tear. That was when she heard it again. Yes, music and laughing, too. Now, where was it coming from? "If you're wondering who is making that dreadful noise," sighed a very slimy snail, sliding along a stalk above her, "then you'd better go down to the old Black Water Pond."

Fairy Isabelle sped towards the pond and, flying out of the trees, she saw an amazing sight. On big lily pads, floating on the water, were all her friends, playing music and singing and laughing. Her mom was putting up a banner between two trees that read, 'Fairy Isabelle Our Best Friend'.

Isabelle's mom flew up, hugged her and said, "I'm sorry, Isabelle, to make you do all those chores, but I had to keep you at home until this wonderful surprise was ready."

Fairy Isabelle
Our Best Friend

"We love you, Isabelle," cheered her friends. "You're the best fairy in all of the forest and this is your party!" They hugged and kissed Isabelle, until she squealed. "Thank you, everyone," said Isabelle, smiling. "This is the best surprise, ever. Let's all dance!" Everyone had a wonderful time. They ate and danced and sang until the sun started to set and then they all went home feeling very happy. None of them, however, were as happy as Isabelle. She definitely wasn't a fed up fairy anymore!

# The Princess and the Lost Crown

Princess Sophie was a bad little girl, who always liked to get her own way. If she wanted ice cream, she had ice cream. If she wanted to wear pink boots, she wore pink boots. Whenever anyone tried to stop her, she would lie on the floor and scream, until the king and queen gave in. One day, Princess Sophie wanted cake for breakfast. The king said no. Just as she started to scream, he said, "Let's go to the beach!"

Princess Sophie loved going to the beach, so she ate her entire breakfast without whining. In no time at all, the royal court was all packed up and on its way to the beach in lots of the royal carriages.

When they arrived, Princess Sophie announced that she wanted to put on her bathing suit. So, a tent was set up and the princess and her maid went inside to change. Everyone else waited outside, nervously.

At last, Princess Sophie came out of the tent, wearing her bathing suit and a little crown. She thought she looked fabulous. She told everyone that she was going to go in the sea. "Oh, Sophie dear," said the queen, a little nervously, "you had better leave your crown here."

Princess Sophie screamed at the queen SO loudly that she went very red in the face. The queen quickly said, "There, there," and the disobedient princess stomped down the beach, still wearing her crown.

The king, in an elegant pair of trunks, along with his butler, followed Sophie to the shore. The princess waded into the water up to her knees. She turned to the king and screamed, "It's too cold! I demand that you make it warmer!"

Just then, a big wave rushed up the beach. The king tried to grab Princess Sophie, but the wave knocked her right off her feet. When she came up again, at first she was spluttering, but that soon turned to screaming.

The whole court held their breath. They could all see that the princess had lost her precious crown. She was going to be so angry!

"I AM WET!" yelled Sophie, putting her hands up to move seaweed from her eyes. It was then that she noticed that her crown was missing.

"MY CROWN!" she squealed. "Where is my crown? Find it. Look for it all of you, or I'll SCREAM ALL DAY!"

So, everyone began to look.

All at once, servants were running everywhere. Boats were launched and fishing nets were thrown into the water. Divers rushed in and swam around, ducking into the waves to see if they could find the crown. The king stood in the water, yelling for people to try harder, but no one seemed able to find the crown.

After quite some time, someone shouted that they had found something and everyone rushed to look, but it was only an old teapot!

**127**

Princess Sophie sat on the sand and sobbed. She loved her crown so much and now it was gone forever. What would her friends say when she told them? She was so upset that even when the queen picked her up and hugged her, she didn't complain. Instead, in between sobs, Princess Sophie mumbled that if she could get her precious crown back, she would never be bad again and would always do what the king and queen told her to do.

Just then, one of the servants shouted, "Look!" He pointed to the rocks on the far shore. Everyone stared in amazement, as a large, orange crab climbed slowly out of the water. On one of his claws was Princess Sophie's missing crown!

The servant was sent to fetch the crown and in no time at all, it was back on Princess Sophie's head. She smiled and hugged her parents and from that day on, she always did as she was told.

# The Mermaid and Nessie

Once upon a time, there lived a sweet, little mermaid named Maggie. Now, usually, merfolk live in the seas and great oceans of the world, but Maggie and lots of other merpeople lived in a very deep lake in Scotland, known as a loch. It was called Loch Ness and its water was fresh, not salty. Mermaid Maggie, her mommy, daddy and her mischievous little brother, Andy, lived in a big cave by a forest of long, green weeds.

At bedtime, the children's daddy often told them a story of a big, scary monster named Nessie, that lived at the bottom of the loch. No one had ever seen Nessie, but lots pretended that they had, just to scare each other. Andy loved to swim up behind Maggie and yell, "Nessie's behind you!" He would laugh when he saw she was scared. Maggie would chase him as he sped away, but she wondered if there really was a Nessie?

Early one morning, Maggie and Andy were sitting at the table by the window eating their breakfast. They were having hot Scotch eggs and delicious fish sticks. "Maggie, dear," called their mommy, "would you come in to the kitchen and get some juice for you and Andy, please?" Maggie swam off and it was then that something very odd happened. A strange-looking creature popped its head through the window and ate Maggie's egg. Andy couldn't believe his eyes!

Suddenly, the creature disappeared. Maggie swam back in, carrying the juice and looked at her empty egg cup. "Andy, you bad boy!" she squealed. "You've eaten my egg." Andy sat with his mouth wide open and his eyes as big as saucers, sputtering. He pointed to the window, but Maggie was too mad to notice. "Mommy," she called, "Andy has eaten my egg!"
Their mommy came in and scolded Andy. It wasn't fair, thought Andy. He always got blamed for everything.

After breakfast, Maggie and Andy set off for school. Maggie was holding a special bubble-balloon that she'd been given for her birthday. It floated above her head on a string of seagrass and she was going to show it to her teacher. Andy wanted to hold it, but Maggie said no. He was looking up at it just as the creature from breakfast stuck its head through the long weed and popped the bubble-balloon with its sharp, little teeth.

The string fell down on Maggie's head and she looked up to see lots of tiny bubbles drifting away. She turned to Andy, who was floating by her side and looking up to where the creature had been. "Andy!" yelled Maggie, "why did you do that? It was my best present!"

With tears in her eyes, she swam away before Andy could say a word and thumped straight into something big and squidgy. That was when the big creature licked her cheek!

For a second, Maggie thought she might scream, but the creature smiled and licked her again. She laughed and swam nearer. "Hello," said Maggie. "Who are you?" She was even more surprised when the creature said, "My name's Nessie. What's yours?" After a second, Maggie replied. "I'm Maggie and this is my little brother, Andy." Andy was floating with his mouth open and was so surprised, he couldn't speak.

"Would you be my friends?" asked Nessie, shyly. "I really like you!"

The two merchildren were thrilled. "We'd love to be your friends,"
said Maggie, and Andy nodded shyly. "Let's play hide-and-seek, shall we?"
So, the three friends swam around and hid and laughed a lot. Suddenly,
Maggie remembered the time. "Would you like to come to school
with us, Nessie?" she asked.

Nessie said, "Yes, please!" and so she swam off to school with Maggie and Andy. There were a few yells and screams, mainly from the teacher, when they arrived, but soon all the merchildren were swimming around Nessie, very excited at having such an unusual friend.

Nessie tried to join them for lessons, but she was too big to fit through the small door. The teacher did allow her to put her head through the classroom window, though and Nessie was very pleased.

Mermaid Maggie, little Andy and all of their friends loved playing with their new friend, Nessie. They would take turns riding on her back as she sped really fast through the water, but it was Maggie who was her very special friend. The two of them went everywhere together. So, if you are ever by Loch Ness and see a strange shape floating by, or hear children laughing and playing, perhaps you might have spotted Nessie and her little friend, Maggie the mermaid.

# The Fairy Who Collected Things

Deep in Crackley Woods, to the right of a very old oak tree, there lived a bright, little fairy named Dora. Her house was a teapot she had rescued from a ditch and her most treasured possession was her handbag. You see, Dora collected things. She couldn't even pass a candy wrapper without scooping it up and popping it in her bag. The only problem was that it always made her late and everyone was getting fed up with her.

One afternoon, her fairy friends, Milly, Jilly and Tilly, waited in the hot sunshine for ages, while Dora tried to squash a big stone into her bag. Dora wouldn't give up. "Do come along, now, Dora," said Jilly, who was losing her temper. "We are really late for the fairy tea party and I am SO very hungry!" But not only were they late, when they arrived, all the food had been eaten! Dora's friends were very upset with her.

The next day, Milly, Jilly and Tilly all flew to Dora's teapot. "We really are very sorry, Dora," said Milly, "but your collecting takes up too much time! Why don't you stop and come and play with us, instead?" Dora was very surprised and a little bit hurt. "But I love collecting," she replied, sadly. "Well, if you change your mind," said Tilly, "we'll be playing by the stream, so you are very welcome to come and join us."

"See you later, Dora," called the fairies, as they flew away. Dora smiled and waved, but inside she felt very sad.

All morning, the sun shone and the birds sang sweetly, but poor Fairy Dora felt miserable. She missed her friends so much. Maybe just a little bit of collecting would make her feel better. She picked up her bag, stepped out of her teapot and set off along the woodland path. Suddenly, Dora thought she could hear someone crying. Just as she rounded a large tree root, she saw who was making all the noise.

Fairy Milly was caught upside down in an old cobweb. She was very frightened and crying very loudly! When she saw Fairy Dora, her face lit up. "Oh, Dora," she sobbed, "please can you help me get out of this mess? I'm really stuck." Dora flew into action, searched through her bag and took out a pair of toy scissors. She then carefully cut the web away and freed her friend. "Thank you so much!" said Milly. "Whatever would I have done without you?"

Further down the forest path, Dora saw a very strange sight. Was that a pair of legs growing in the ground? When she got closer, Dora saw it was Fairy Jilly, stuck, head first in a rabbit hole. "What happened?" asked Dora. "I dropped my wand down here and now I'm stuck," wept Jilly. "Can you pull me out, please, Dora?"

Dora found some string in her bag, tied it around Jilly's feet and pulled. Soon, Jilly was free. She gave Dora a big hug.

Dora suddenly heard an angry buzzing. She flew quickly towards the noise. She found some angry bees and Fairy Tilly, who was firmly stuck in a pool of honey by a beehive. "Oh, Dora," sobbed Tilly. "I only wanted a little honey for tea and now I'm trapped. Please get me out!"

Dora swished the bees away with her wand, then pulled Tilly out and wiped her feet with a cloth from her bag. Tilly was so grateful.

Each of the three fairies was very glad that Dora was still their friend. Without her and the things in her wonderful bag, they would still be stuck. "Dora," said Fairy Milly, "we wish we knew how to thank you!" "Well, I have an idea," said Dora. "Here are three bags just like mine. Now, you can help me carry all my bits and pieces." The fairies agreed and soon they flew away, with their bags full of Dora's things. Dora was very happy and no one teased her about collecting things ever again!

# The Ghost Princess

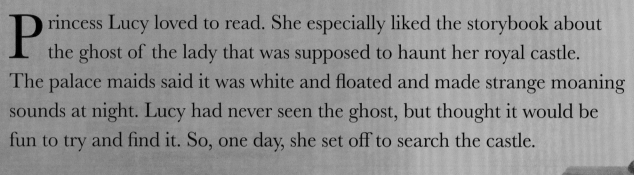

Princess Lucy loved to read. She especially liked the storybook about the ghost of the lady that was supposed to haunt her royal castle. The palace maids said it was white and floated and made strange moaning sounds at night. Lucy had never seen the ghost, but thought it would be fun to try and find it. So, one day, she set off to search the castle.

Lucy couldn't see the ghost anywhere. By the time she got to the attic, she was very tired and flopped down for a few minutes on a dusty and very old trunk. After she got her breath back, Lucy wondered what was inside the trunk, so she hopped off and lifted the lid. Well, inside were lots of interesting things. She pulled out a dusty spinning top, a tennis ball and a toy rabbit and then, she saw something wonderful.

It was a white dress, just like they used to wear in the olden days. "Cool," thought Lucy, "I can play dress up." She carefully took the dress out of the trunk and began pulling it over her head. The dress was wide and very long and the last bit snagged on her crown. It was then that things started to go wrong. Princess Lucy tugged and pulled, but the more she did it, the more the dress stuck. Suddenly, Princess Lucy tripped.

She fumbled through the doorway and stumbled down the stairs.
The little princess couldn't see a thing. The collar hid her face completely,
but she didn't hurt herself at all, because the dress was so big. The one
thing she couldn't do was stop!

Just as she flew around a corner, sleeves flapping around her like great,
ghostly wings, a door opened and a maid came out, carrying a vase
of flowers. She thought Princess Lucy was the ghost and screamed.

Princess Lucy tried to tell her that she was trapped inside the dress, but all that came out was, "Ooh-ooh-ooh-ooh!" as she boinged from step to step. That only caused the maid to scream even louder and off she ran.

On the next landing, the snooty butler was walking by with a tray of tea. Princess Lucy gave him such a fright, he threw the tea tray in the air and it landed with an enormous CRASH!

Princess Lucy tried to say she was very sorry, but all that came out was,
"WHOO-WHOO-WHOO-WHOO!" as she shot past, getting faster
all the time. She was feeling dizzy and wished she could stop. That might
have happened if the page boy, who was standing on the stairs, was just
a little fatter, but he wasn't. Princess Lucy knocked him over like a bowling
pin. He sat up just in time to see her flying past and screamed, "Ghost!"

Princess Lucy couldn't see and she couldn't hear, but she was sure that she would reach the hall soon. In fact, she was almost there, but the worst was yet to come. The pastry cook was just coming out of a door, carrying a huge cake. As Princess Lucy arrived in the hall at top speed, she bowled him right over. The beautiful cake shot in the air and landed in a heap on the floor.

Princess Lucy rolled across the floor and stopped still. Everyone in the castle had come to the hall to see what all the fuss was about, even the king and queen. Then, the white dress moved. First a hand appeared, followed by an ear and then an eye. Finally, Princess Lucy stood up and stumbled from the dress.

The king smiled. "It's not the ghost," he said. "It's just Princess Lucy." Everyone was very relieved, they'd had enough of ghosts for one day!

# The Mermaid Who Wanted to Fly

A long time ago, Ellie the mermaid sat upon a rock in a faraway sea. She noticed a little crab had its claw stuck in a crack in the rock and she gently helped it back into the water. Suddenly, a whoosh made her turn and there, before her eyes, was the most beautiful, pink fish and it was actually flying! Ellie held her breath as she watched it glide through the air and finally, splash into the water again.

Ellie was amazed. She had never seen anything so wonderful before in her life. Suddenly, another pink fish flew out of the water, followed by two more. They seemed to glide for ages in the air and then slip softly back into the sea. Oh, how Ellie wanted to fly like that! She slipped off the rock, dived under the water and looked around. There, below her, she could see the pink fish, diving down deep. She flicked her tail and swam after them.

"Oh, fish," she called, loudly, "please wait for me!" The fish stopped and turned around. Ellie swam up and said, "Please, dear fish, will you teach me how to fly, just like you?" The fish looked at each other and then the largest replied, "You're too big, little mermaid and you don't have wings like us." Ellie glanced down and she saw that the fish did in fact have fins like wings. She stared at her own sides and saw only her arms.

It was then that she had an idea. "Please, fish, will you return here tomorrow and if by then I have wings, will you teach me to fly?" The fish all huddled together and whispered.

At last, the biggest fish swam up to Ellie and said, "We will be here tomorrow when the sun is highest in the sky. If you have managed to grow wings, we will certainly teach you how to fly." Then, they turned and swam away.

Ellie was so excited. She swam to a bed of really strong seaweed and began to pull up long strands. When she had plenty, she sped off to the rocks where the tiny crabs lived. "Little crabs," she called, softly, "I need to make some wings. Will you please help me?"

One crab squeaked, "Little mermaid, you helped our friend when he was stuck, so now we are more than happy to help you."

The crabs scuttled across to the pile of seaweed and quickly got to work. The smallest crabs wove the fine strands together and the biggest crabs snipped off the ends with their sharp claws.

They worked for hours and hours and at last, Ellie slipped her arms into a pair of shiny, green wings. She waved them back and forth and they slid through the water with ease. Ellie was so excited!

So, when the sun rose high in the sky, Ellie was sitting on the same rock, waiting for the flying fish. Suddenly, they flew out of the water, calling, "Come and join us!" and Ellie dived in. For several hours, they showed Ellie what to do. She had to swim down deep and then suddenly speed up to the surface. At the final second, she had to flick her wings. At last, after many tries, she found herself sailing through the air.

Ellie loved flying. She practiced every day with the flying fish beside her. She grew stronger and soon she stayed in the air for longer. Then, one evening, she flicked her tail very hard as she left the water and beat her winged arms and she was really flying, leaving the amazed fish behind! So, if one day you are sitting on a rock by the sea and you think you see a flying mermaid, it just might be Ellie!

# Princess Polly's Birthday Party

In a castle high on a hill, there lived a little girl named Princess Polly. It was soon to be her birthday, but who was she going to invite to her party? Her castle was far away from other kingdoms. She didn't know any other princes or princesses and that made her a little sad. So, Polly decided that she would go on a walk around the castle to see if that would cheer her up.

In the hall, Polly heard someone laughing. It was a little girl. "Who are you?" asked Princess Polly.

"My name is Anna, Your Highness and my mom is the royal dressmaker," said the girl. "Please come and see what my mom has made."

Princess Polly stepped into the room and there was the most beautiful dress she had ever seen. "Oh, I would love a dress like that," she said.

The little girl smiled. "Maybe one day, Your Highness."

Just then, a boy ran past the door. The princess stopped him and asked him who he was and why he was running so fast. He bowed very low and said, "My name is Joseph, Your Highness, and I am taking a message from the queen to my father, who is the royal shoemaker. The queen has a very special order for him and I must run, or my father won't have time to make the shoes!" He bowed again and ran off.

Princess Polly was hungry, so she went to the kitchen for a snack. As she walked in the door, she saw two little girls, who were helping a lady mix something in a bowl. "Who are you?" she asked. "We are Jenny and Penny, Your Highness," said the oldest girl. "We are making a cake with our mommy, the royal cook." The princess sniffed and said it smelled delicious. She said she would love some cake and the girls smiled.

After her snack, Princess Polly went for a walk in the royal gardens.
She saw a man and a little boy working in a flower bed. "Who are you?"
she asked the boy.

"I am Thomas," said the boy, with a smile, "and this is my father, the
royal gardener. We have grown these beautiful roses."

The princess sniffed a rose and her face lit up. "They are really wonderful,"
she said. "I would love to have some of those."

That night, Princess Polly didn't sleep very well because she was worried that she would have a birthday party with no guests. It was terrible!

Polly awoke with a start. She had just had the most wonderful idea! She would invite Anna and Joseph and Jenny and Penny and Thomas to her party! And that was when she noticed a beautiful, yellow dress by her bed and a pair of gold shoes on the floor. She jumped out of bed and put them on.

Polly ran through the palace, calling out the children's names. When they came to her, she invited them all to her birthday party. They jumped up and down and cheered with excitement!

That afternoon, Princess Polly had her birthday party, wearing the dress made by the royal dressmaker and the shoes made by the royal shoemaker. The tables were decorated with lovely pink roses, grown by the royal gardener and there was a magnificent cake, made by the royal cook.

"Thank you all for coming," said the princess. "I love my new dress and shoes. The roses are just what I wanted and I can't wait to eat my cake. Dive in, everyone!"

After eating cake, they played party games. Princess Polly won at musical chairs and Thomas won the game of hide-and-seek. Everyone laughed, danced and ate more birthday cake until it was time for bed. Thanks to her new friends, this was the best birthday Polly had ever had!

# The Fairy Who Sneezed a Lot

Once upon a time, there lived a sweet little fairy named Fairy Flutter. One sunny morning, she flew out of her house and suddenly sneezed. It was a really big sneeze, the sort that makes you spin in the air, and that's when the trouble started, for in front of Flutter was a very large, angry frog … and he was PINK! Fairy Flutter sneezed again and he turned BLUE. She had sneezed him BLUE! "Oh, goodness!" she cried, in alarm. "However did that happen?"

She flew away until she came to a small stream. Swimming on the water was a duck and her tiny ducklings. "Oh, Mrs. Duck," she cried, "you will never guess what just happened! I came out of my house and…" then she knew she was going to sneeze, ACHOOO!

She sneezed all over the ducks and suddenly, they'd grown three times as big! Fairy Flutter burst into tears and flew off, as fast as her pretty little wings could carry her.

Fairy Flutter flew so fast that she didn't see a huge rabbit until it was too late. She bumped into his furry tummy and tumbled onto the ground. Fairy Flutter looked up at his face and ATISHOOOO! Suddenly, the rabbit's ears shrank until you could hardly see them.

He didn't look happy at all. "Now look here, little fairy," he shouted. "What have you done to my ears?" Fairy Flutter stared in shock, plopped down onto a stone and started to cry.

That was where the Fairy Queen found her. "Poor, little Flutter," said the queen, kindly. "Why are you crying?" The little fairy looked up and told the Fairy Queen all about the frog, ducks and the rabbit. When she had finished, they saw that the frog, ducks and rabbit were right by them, looking very upset. "Look up into the air, Flutter," said the Fairy Queen. "It's the pollen drifting about that is making you sneeze so much!"

The Fairy Queen raised her wand and flicked it towards the animals. They instantly returned to their normal selves and scurried away. "When a fairy sneezes," said the Fairy Queen, "all sorts of strange things can happen. You must always carry a handkerchief and sneeze into that!" She gave Flutter a lace handkerchief. "Thank you, Your Majesty," said Flutter, with a smile. "You always make things right!" The Fairy Queen laughed and hugged Fairy Flutter and with that they flew happily away.